Snow Day!

Werner Zimmermann

Scholastic Canada Ltd.

Toronto New York London Auckland Sydney
Mexico City New Delhi Hong Kong Buenos Aires

Dedicated to my sons, Christopher and Tristan;
to the memory of their mother; and to the fine old house
on Glasgow Street that welcomed and sheltered us all.
— W.Z.

The illustrations in this book were painted in watercolour on Arches paper.
The type was set in 22 point Garamond.

This book has been printed on chlorine-free paper made with 10% post-consumer waste.

Scholastic Canada Ltd.
604 King Street West, Toronto, Ontario M5V 1E1, Canada

Scholastic Inc.
557 Broadway, New York, NY 10012, USA

Scholastic Australia Pty Limited
PO Box 579, Gosford, NSW 2250, Australia

Scholastic New Zealand Limited
Private Bag 94407, Botany, Manukau 2163, New Zealand

Scholastic Children's Books
Euston House, 24 Eversholt Street, London NW1 1DB, UK

Library and Archives Canada Cataloguing in Publication
Zimmermann, H. Werner (Heinz Werner), 1951-
Snow day / Werner Zimmermann.
Originally published: Markham, Ont. : North Winds, 1999.

ISBN 978-0-439-95710-6
I. Title.
PS8599.I463S66 2007   jC813'.54   C2007-902212-X

ISBN-10 0-439-95710-9

6 5 4 3   Printed in Canada   114   11 12 13 14

Something woke us early that morning.
Maybe it was the silence.

Millions of snowflakes drifted down.
Everything was covered in a deep
blanket of snow.

Would it be deep enough?
Would school be closed?
We waited and waited.

I was just about to
drag myself out the
door when we heard
the magic words . . .

Snow Day!

7

My friends were already outside.
We threw ourselves into the snow, making angels and catching flakes with our tongues.
Mupps did too.

People were digging out their cars. The big kids were going to clear walks for the old people, so we grabbed our shovels and followed.

But our way was blocked by a
huge train pushing through the
snow. It wouldn't give up, and
neither would our neighbour.

We waved as the snowplow
rumbled up the road.
The grownups didn't.
Mupps just barked.

After lunch we headed
for the park for hockey
and tag. The old maple
was Home Free.

Mupps didn't know
who was It, so he chased
everyone.

He even chased the puck!
Our fingers and toes were
frozen, and our pants were
soaked from falling down,
but nobody cared.

On the way home we passed
fantastic snow blocks. We just
couldn't leave them behind.
They'd be great for . . .

a snow fort!

It had a roof and a flag and a tunnel for a door. It was the greatest snow fort ever. Mupps helped. So did Mouse, our cat.

Our faces were stinging by the time Mom called us in. She gave us hot chocolate. We told her about our fort.

When our clothes were dry, we headed
back out to build a MONSTER slide.
   Mouse watched from the fence, where
it was safe.

By suppertime we could hardly keep our eyes open. Outside, more snow was beginning to fall.

Just before bed we had one last look.
Millions and millions of flakes were falling.
We fell asleep hoping for only one thing . . .
another Snow Day.